THE SECRET SANTA MYSTERY

By Gail Herman

Illustrated by Duendes del Sur

SCHOLASTIC INC.

New York Toronto London Auckland Sydney
Mexico City New Delhi Hong Kong Buenos Aires

ISBN 0-439-45619-3

15 14 13 12   40   11 12/0

Designed by Maria Stasavage
Printed in the U.S.A.
First printing, November 2002

Snow fell.

The wind blew.

Scooby-Doo, Shaggy, and the gang drove up to a cottage in the woods.

Everyone jumped out of the van.
Daphne sighed. "What a nice place to
spend the holiday!"

"Just smell the fresh air!" Velma added.

Shaggy and Scooby sniffed. "Fresh doughnuts smell better," said Shaggy.

"This Christmas will be great," Fred promised. "Let's start with a hike in the woods!"

Shaggy eyed the bags of food. "Like, you guys go. Scoob and I will bring everything inside."

"Don't forget the Secret Santa presents!" said Daphne.

"I remember the Secret Santa presents!" said Shaggy. "We each picked a name out of a hat. Then we bought a present for that person. But it's a big secret. So, like, no one knows who they're getting a present from!"

"No. I mean don't forget to bring the presents inside." Daphne pointed into the van. "They are in that big bag."

Then she, Fred, and Velma headed into the woods.

"Let's get grooving, good buddy," said Shaggy. He picked up one of the grocery bags. "Hmmm. That's heavy. Let's make it a little lighter."

He tossed chips, an apple pie, and a
hamburger to Scooby.
Gulp, gulp, gulp.
They were gone in a flash.
"Rummy!"

Shaggy picked up another bag.
"Like, this one's heavy, too," he said. In a
little while, Shaggy and Scooby were full.
But the bags were almost empty.

"Oops!" said Shaggy. "There's no food left for Christmas dinner! What are we going to do?"

Scooby wagged his tail. "Ropen resents?"

"Great idea. Let's open presents!"

Shaggy and Scooby trooped back to the van.

"What happened?" cried Shaggy.

The Secret Santa bag was ripped open. Torn wrapping paper was everywhere. And all the presents were gone!

"Zoinks!" cried Shaggy. "Somebody was here!"

"*Rrrrrr!*" A loud roar filled the woods.

"Or rome*thing*!" said Scooby.

Shaggy pointed to giant footprints in the snow.

"These are monster footprints!" Shaggy cried. "A monster with legs and legs and more legs!"

"We have no food. And now a monster has our presents!" Shaggy's eyes widened in horror.

"We got a cookbook for Velma! With great dessert recipes in it! Follow those footprints!"

Shaggy and Scooby tracked the prints. Suddenly, they stopped.

They heard growling.

"*Rrrrrr!*"

They peered through the branches. There it was! The giant monster!

It was white from head to toe!
It was as wide as it was tall.
"A snow monster!" cried Shaggy. "We have
to tell the others!"

They turned to run. But something had caught them.

It grabbed Shaggy's scarf.

It grabbed Scooby's scarf, too.

They couldn't move.

"Let go of us, Snow Monster!" Shaggy shouted.

"Snow Monster? It's only us," said Fred.

"But there is a Snow Monster!" Shaggy said. "It has all our presents! And it will want us next!"

"Our presents are gone?" Fred turned to Daphne sadly. "I got you a comb and brush," he said.

"I got you a hat and mittens," Velma said to Fred.

"We got Velma a cookbook," said Shaggy.

Daphne looked at Shaggy and Scooby. "I made Snooby Snacks for you two. More than you have ever seen!"

Scooby Snacks!

"We're going after that monster!" Shaggy cried.

"Right!" said Scooby.

The two buddies crashed through the trees.

Velma started after them. "No, wait!" she
said. "I can see it. It's not a monster. It's a —"

"Mother bear and her cubs!" Shaggy said.

"We saw them on our hike," Velma said.

"They're eating our Snooby Snacks!" said Shaggy.

"Wearing my hat and mittens," Fred said. "Using my comb and brush," said Daphne. "Ripping pages from my cookbook to make a place to sleep!" said Velma. "They are getting ready to sleep through winter."

Daphne smiled. "The bears need our presents. So let's leave them."

"Ro Recret Ranta?" said Scooby.

"Like, think again, good buddy," Shaggy told him. "We're all Secret Santas — for the bears!"

The gang was happy about the presents.
"We'll tell everyone about dinner later,"
Shaggy whispered to Scooby.

Back at the cottage, Velma opened all the cabinets. Then she checked the refrigerator. Finally she looked in the grocery bags. "Where's the food?" she asked.

"Um, um, um . . ." Shaggy said.

"Rum, rum, rum," Scooby added.

They backed into the dining room. And there, on the table, was a whole Christmas dinner.

Whoosh! Shaggy and Scooby heard a noise
by the fireplace.

They spun around — just in time to see a
boot disappearing up the chimney.

They had a Secret Santa, too!

"Rappy Rolidays!"